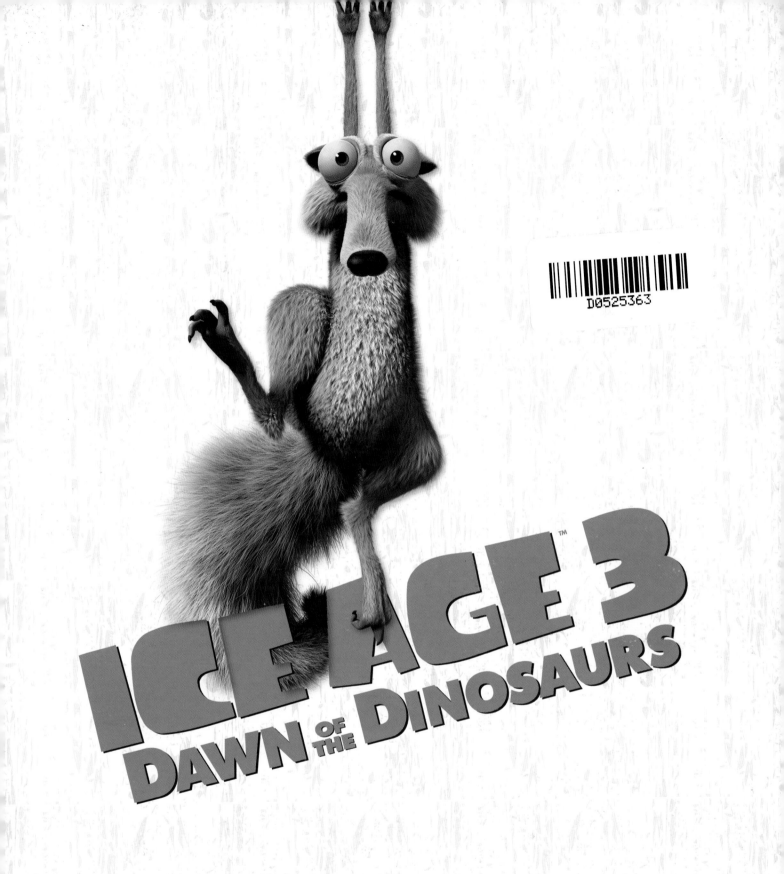

ICE AGE 3
DAWN OF THE DINOSAURS

The Movie Storybook

Dawn of the Dinosaurs TM and © 2009 Twentieth Century Fox Film Corporation. All Rights Reserved.

First published in the UK by HarperCollins Children's Books in 2009

1 3 5 7 9 10 8 6 4 2

ISBN: 978-0-00-731080-7

www.harpercollins.co.uk

ICE AGE 3™
DAWN OF THE DINOSAURS

The Movie Storybook

Adapted by Layla Rose

HarperCollins *Children's Books*

Everyone in the Valley was excited. The mammoths Ellie and Manny were going to have a baby! Ellie couldn't wait to be a mum, but Manny was more than just excited. He was a nervous wreck!

Manny was building a playground for the baby. It was perfect and very safe. He drained the pond, padded the sharp tree branches, and even stuck a snowball on a bird's sharp beak!

Ellie loved the playground, but when she saw how everything had been baby-proofed, she sighed. "Manny, you've got to relax," she said. "The best way to protect our baby is to have all of our friends around us." Then Ellie realised someone was missing.

"Wait – where's Diego?" she asked.

Diego was leaping across the plains, chasing a gazelle. He ran hard, pumping his legs with all his might. He inched closer and closer to the gazelle – and suddenly stopped.

Diego was out of breath and couldn't run any further. He wasn't the same lean, mean sabre-toothed tiger he used to be.

The big cat started to think that living in a pack wasn't right for him. He went to the playground to talk to Manny.

"I've been thinking that it might be time for me to head out on my own,"
Diego said. "Having a family is your adventure, not mine."

Manny was hurt. "Well, then go find some adventure, Mr. Adventure Guy,"
he snapped.

Sid the sloth ran up to his fighting friends.

"Stop!" he cried. "This should be the best time of our lives! We're having a baby!"

"No, Sid," said Diego. "*They're* having a baby."

"But we're a herd . . . a family," Sid insisted.

"Face it, Sid," Diego said. "It's time to move on." Diego walked off alone.

Sid felt sad about his herd breaking up. He went for a walk, too.
Suddenly, the ground beneath him cracked, and Sid fell through the
ice into an underground chamber! There he found three eggs sitting
all alone.

"I know what it's like to feel abandoned," Sid said to the eggs. Instead of leaving them where he found them, Sid decided to take the eggs home. He didn't stop to think about their mum and how she would miss them. He wanted them to be *his* children when they hatched.

One by one, Sid carried and rolled the eggs home – but one got away from him! It slid across the ice and went flying towards the jagged rocks. Luckily, Ellie caught it at the last second!

"Sid, you're not meant to be a parent," Manny said. "One of those eggs almost became an omelette!"

"Someone's probably worried sick looking for them," Ellie added.

Sid hadn't thought about what would hatch out of the eggs. The next morning he was shocked to find three broken eggs . . . and three baby *dinosaurs*! Even though they were just born, they were already as big as the sloth, but Sid didn't mind. He was just excited to be a parent. He played peek-a-boo with the dinos and sang songs to them.

Sid took the kids to Manny's new playground. Things quickly got out of control! Manny was angry to find his playground destroyed by the dinosaurs.

"Those kids don't belong here, Sid!" Manny cried. "Wherever you found them, take them back."

"I'm not getting rid of my kids," Sid said.

Suddenly, the ground began to rumble. A giant Tyrannosaurus rex burst up through the ground with a roar! She stomped right over to Sid and the little dinosaurs. It was clear that she was the mother of the smaller dinos – they looked just like her! She scooped them all up in her mouth – including Sid – and charged back down the hole.

"Heeeelp!" cried Sid.

Ellie wasted no time in following the dinosaur underground. Their friend was in trouble!

Manny, Crash, and Eddie followed her and found themselves in a cave. Walking around, they realised they were on a cliff. Looking over the edge of the cliff, everyone gasped. Below them stretched a green leafy jungle, where dinosaurs roamed free. There was no snow or ice in sight!

"We've been living above an entire world and we didn't even *know* it," Ellie said in surprise.

The gang was surprised to find Diego in the jungle as well.
"Diego? What are you doing down here?" Manny asked.
"I'm looking for Sid, same as you," Diego replied. "I heard his cry for help."
Before the friends could talk more, an enormous dinosaur with a huge spiked tail rose up in front of them and growled! The gang ran for their lives, but they ran right into another pack of ferocious dinosaurs. They were surrounded!

Out of nowhere, the group heard a strange yell. "Fire in the hole!" screamed a weasel, who appeared suddenly, swinging on a vine. With great speed and stealth, the weasel threw one fruit bomb after another at the dinosaurs. Huge clouds of smoke billowed around them. When the smoke cleared, everyone was safe!

"I'm Buck. Short for Buckminster, long for Buh," said the weasel. "What are you guys doing here?"

"Our friend Sid was taken by a dinosaur," explained Crash.

"You'd better watch out down here," Buck warned them. "What are you going to do when you run into the BEAST? I call him . . . Rudy!"

"Now let's move out," Buck said. As they followed the weasel through the jungle, Manny stopped to pick some fruit, but vines from a giant flower wrapped around his leg. The mammoth looked down and said to his friends, "The pretty flower is squeezing me!"

Diego laughed at him until the vines also grabbed his leg, and lifted both animals up into the air! The vines dangled the two friends over the flower as the petals opened and it prepared to eat them. Luckily, Buck knew just what to do and swiftly got them down.

That night around the campfire, Buck told them about his most dangerous battle ever: the time he fought Rudy the dinosaur! Rudy had swallowed the weasel whole, and Buck thought he was finished. In the end, Buck walked away with his life, *and* one of Rudy's teeth!

Meanwhile, Sid was having his own adventure. Momma T. rex had carried Sid and the kids back to her home. Now that the young dinos were safe, she was about to sink her teeth into the sloth, but the kids rushed to Sid's defence.

"Grrr!" growled one of the kids. Another dinosaur bared his teeth.

"See, the kids have spoken!" said Sid. Momma snorted.

From then on, Sid and Momma decided to work together to raise the little dinosaurs, but it wasn't easy. When Momma brought home a bird for the kids, Sid refused to let them eat it.

"I've raised them vegetarian," he said.

Suddenly, a terrifying roar echoed in their ears. Momma T. rex knew it was the sound of Rudy, the terrifying and toothy beast Buck had battled long ago! She grabbed everyone – even Sid – and *ran.*

"AAAAAAAAAHH!!!" Sid screamed.

Nearby, Sid's friends heard his terrified scream.
"Sid and Rudy must be over by the lava falls," said Buck.
"We'll have to move fast."

Ellie was moving slowly and fell behind the rest of the group. She stopped for a moment to rest, and realised what was happening to her. From atop a pile of boulders, Ellie called out to Manny, who was already down below.

"The baby's coming!" Ellie shouted. Manny stopped in his tracks and turned around.

"We're coming, Ellie!" Manny yelled back to Ellie as he tried to climb up to her.

"There's only one thing to do," Buck said. "Possums, you're with me. Manny, you take care of Ellie until we get back."

"What? No! No, you can't leave now!" cried Manny. "She's – you have to – "

"It's all right," Diego said. "I've got your back."

As they climbed up to meet Ellie, Manny and Diego saw a pack of large, ferocious guanlong dinosaurs heading their way. The friends looked at each other. They knew they had to keep Ellie safe. "All right, let's do it." Manny nodded. Manny and Diego sprang into action and faced off against the horde of guanlongs, but they were soon surrounded. The friends began fighting their way back to Ellie.

Meanwhile, Sid was dealing with his own dinosaur problem. He was separated from the T. rex family and Rudy was hot on his trail.

"Shoo, go away!" Sid cried out, but Rudy wouldn't give up. Sid looked ahead and realised there was a river of lava coming towards him! Soon it surrounded the rock he was standing on. There was nowhere to go!

Luckily, Buck soared out of the cliffs on a pterodactyl, with the possums hanging on. Just before the lava flowed over Sid's rock, Buck pulled the pterodactyl upright and grabbed Sid in his talons just in time.

Meanwhile, Ellie was about to have her baby! Diego was at her side, fighting off any creature that tried to come near them.

"Can I hold your paw?" asked Ellie.

"Of course," said Diego as he smoothly knocked another dinosaur off the cliff.

Manny had just a few more dinos to fight off before he could get to Ellie. He was ready for them! Mustering up all of his might, Manny slammed into a tree that was holding up a group of rocks. The rocks tumbled down the cliff, creating an avalanche. The dinosaurs retreated. Manny had stopped them!

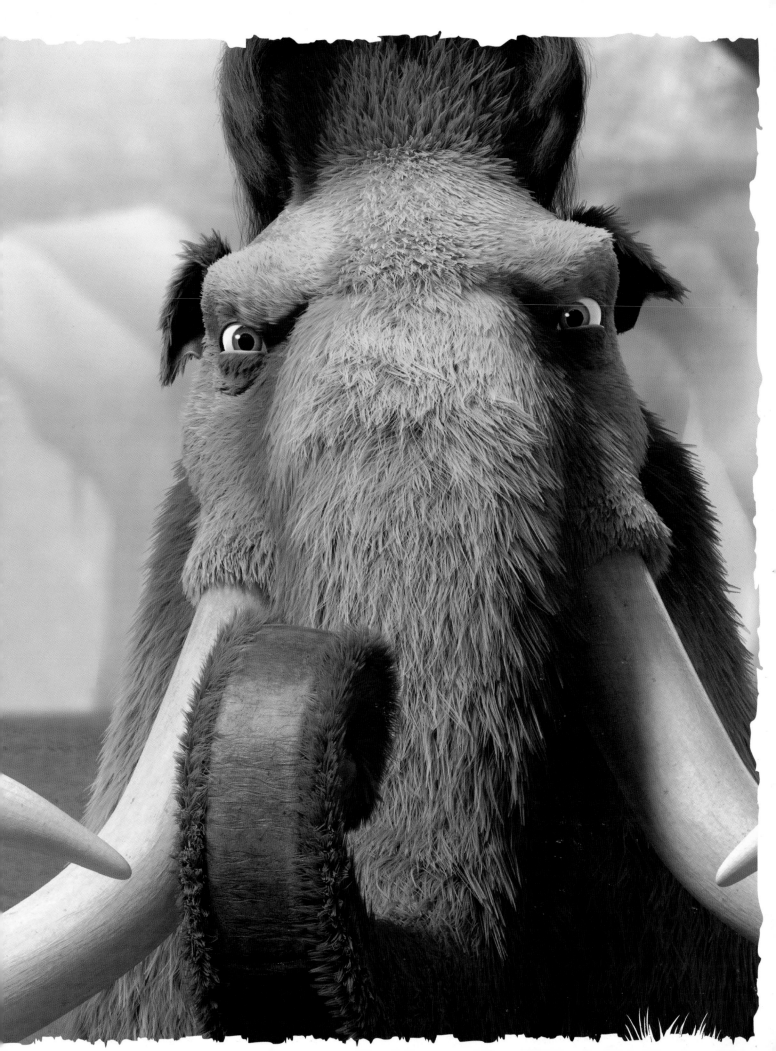

"Waaaah!" Manny reached Ellie just as he heard the cry of his newborn baby mammoth. He couldn't believe all that had just happened. "You did good," he told Ellie. "*We* did good," she said.

"Incoming!" called Sid. He was approaching fast on the pterodactyl with Buck and the possums, Crash and Eddie. When Sid landed, he took one look at the new baby and said, "She looks just like her mother! Thank goodness! No offence, Manny. You're beautiful on the inside."

Everyone was happy to have Sid back.

As the friends started their journey back home, it grew very dark. It took them a moment to realise that the sun was blocked by an enormous creature with greyish-white skin, big claws, and giant teeth! It was Rudy!

The huge dinosaur roared. Then the gang heard more thundering footsteps behind them. It was Momma and the dinosaur kids to the rescue! Momma T. rex gave Rudy a big shove and knocked him over. Buck tied up Rudy's snout with a vine before the vicious dino could get back up, and then Momma knocked Rudy over a cliff.

"Oh, thank you, Momma!" Sid cried as he gave her a big hug. "Take good care of our kids." Then he gave his dinosaur family one last hug and ran to join his friends.

The possums invited Buck to go home with them, but as they made their way back through the cave, the weasel heard a familiar *ROAR* vibrate through the air. It was Rudy! He must have got loose and climbed back up the cliff.

Buck stopped. The call of the wild was too strong – he knew he was destined to battle Rudy again. With a wave goodbye the weasel disappeared back into the jungle.

"Welcome to the Ice Age, sweetie," Ellie said to their baby as they reached the tundra.

So much had happened, but now they were back in the Valley and everything felt normal again. Diego promised his friends that he wouldn't be leaving any time soon.

The pack was back together at last.